DRAGONS
AND
MONSTERS

DRAGONS AND MONSTERS

FOLK TALES FROM AROUND THE WORLD

RETOLD BY ANITA GANERI
ILLUSTRATED BY ALAN BAKER

MACDONALD YOUNG BOOKS

This edition first published in Great Britain in 1996 by
Macdonald Young Books an imprint of Wayland Publishers Limited
61 Western Road
Hove
East Sussex
BN3 1JD

For Chris

Designed by Joy FitzSimmons
Edited by Nicola Barber
Printed and bound in Portugal by Edições ASA

British Library Cataloguing in Publication Data

Ganeri, Anita
    Dragons and monsters
    1. Children's stories, English
    I. Title
    823.9′14[J]

ISBN 0 7500 18143

CONTENTS

INTRODUCTION

This book will take you on a journey into strange and fabulous lands inhabited by fire-breathing dragons, fearsome monsters and extraordinary mythical beasts. The stories collected in this book come from all over the world – from China, Africa, Australia, Greece, Scandinavia, Ireland and England. Some may be familiar and some will be new, but all of them draw on a magnificent mixture of myth, legend and truth. So settle down for a good read about friendly (and not-so-friendly!) dragons, menacing sea serpents, wicked witches, hungry dwarves, fiery giants, and, last but not least, the cunning creature known as Mantis who stole the fire and nearly got away with it.

THE DRAGON BOY'S PEARL

In Chinese legend, dragons ruled the sea and the life-giving rain clouds and were thought to be very lucky. Many Chinese dragon stories are thousands of years old. This is the story of how a boy became a dragon.

Long ago, a boy lived with his mother in a small village by the banks of a river in China. The family was very poor. To earn a living, the boy sold bundles of freshly cut grass to the other villagers. The villagers fed the grass to their animals. The boy didn't make much money – just enough for him and his mother to live on, if they scrimped and saved.

One summer, disaster struck. No rain fell for weeks on end and a terrible drought turned the land to dust. The river ran dry; the grass shrivelled and died. The boy had to search far and wide to find some green grass to sell. When, at last, he found a patch that seemed somehow to have escaped the drought, he cut as much as he could carry and hurried home as fast as fire. Every day after that he returned to the patch and cut more of the grass, which always grew back fresh and green. But the grass was a long way from the boy's village and his daily journey there and back left him feeling very weary. Then he had a brilliant idea.

'I know,' he said. 'I'll dig up a clump of grass and replant it in my garden.'

And this is what he did. Next day, he took his spade and dug a big clump of the fresh, green grass. But as he lifted the clump out of the ground he nearly fell over in astonishment. For, in the hole left by the clump of grass lay a huge, round, gleaming white pearl. It was the most beautiful thing the boy had ever seen. Very carefully, he picked up the pearl and put it in his pocket. Then, clutching his spade and the clump of grass, he set off for home.

The boy planted the grass in his garden, full of hope and high spirits. Then he showed the pearl to his mother.

'It's so beautiful,' she said, gazing at it in wonder, 'and it must be extremely valuable. I'll hide it in this empty rice jar to keep it safe while we decide what to do with it.'

When the boy went to inspect his garden the next day, his spirits fell. Despite his best efforts, the grass had withered and died.

'What shall we do now?' he complained to his mother. 'How will we manage? We can't even afford to buy any food.'

'Don't worry,' she replied. 'The pearl will help us, I'm sure of it.'

Sure enough, when she opened the rice jar, it was full to the brim with rice. The boy and his mother looked at each other. If the pearl was indeed magical, their days of hardship were over. They placed the pearl in their money jar, with the last few coins they owned. When they looked in the morning, the jar was full of money!

The boy and his mother kept their pearl a closely-guarded secret. But people soon noticed that their fortunes had changed. They wore new clothes, and put on weight. They bought new furniture, and a fine horse. It was all very suspicious. Rumours quickly spread, and one day thieves broke into the house while the boy and his mother were inside. One by one, the thieves

looked into all the jars on the shelf. But before the thieves reached the money jar in which the pearl was hidden, the boy snatched the jar off the shelf, grabbed the pearl from inside and popped it straight into his mouth.

The boy swallowed the pearl. A strange burning feeling began to spread through him, from the tips of his toes to the hairs on his head. He ran to the river and drank and drank, gulping down water as fast as he could. But still he burned with the terrible fire. Then his body began to change. He grew bigger. His eyes bulged and popped. His skin became covered in golden-green scales. Horns grew from his head and wings sprouted from his back. Right in front of his mother's eyes, the boy turned into a dragon.

The dragon dived into the river, ready to swim off to a new, watery home. He turned his long neck and gave his mother a fond farewell glance. As he did so, the skies opened and a mighty downpour of rain fell on the parched land. The drought was over, thanks to the dragon boy and his magic pearl.

ST GEORGE AND THE DRAGON

This is the story of St George, the patron saint of England, and his famous victory over a fire-breathing, child-eating dragon. The story symbolises the triumph of good over evil.

Long ago, the city of Silene in northern Africa was terrorised by a huge, hideous dragon that made its home on the banks of a deep lake at the edge of town. The dragon had an enormous appetite, and it munched its way through a great many of the sheep and goats that grazed on the slopes near its lair. One day, however, the townspeople found the grisly remains of a shepherd boy. The dragon had obviously eaten the boy for dinner. From then on, the dragon developed quite a taste for people and came right up to the city gates in the hope of catching someone unawares. To keep him happy, every day the townspeople left two sheep by the side of the lake. But soon there were no sheep left, nor goats, nor pigs . . .

The townspeople were faced with a dreadful dilemma. What could they feed to the dragon? The mayor and his council had no choice.

'We will have to feed the dragon with children,' the mayor announced. 'Lots will be drawn to decide each day's victim.'

And so it happened. One day, the name of the king's daughter was pulled out of the hat. The king was appalled and pleaded with the mayor to spare her life.

'She's the only daughter I've got,' he begged and sobbed. 'Please don't send her to be eaten.'

His pleas fell on deaf ears. The princess was duly taken down to the lake and tied to a tree. She screamed and screamed but it seemed that nothing could save her.

Now, it so happened that just at that moment a knight in shiny, silver armour came riding by the lake. His name was George; his mission to fight evil wherever he found it. George heard the princess's screams and galloped over to find her.

'Have no fear, princess,' he cried. 'I will save you!'

'Oh no,' she sobbed, 'leave me here. If the dragon catches you trying to help me, he'll kill you too.'

But George had no intention of leaving the princess to her fate. The dragon was about to get rather more than he'd bargained for! George rode his horse straight down to the water's edge, pulled out his sword and issued this brave challenge:

'Come out and fight, vile dragon, or stay away from this place for ever!'

The surface of the lake began to smoke and steam, then the waters parted with a thunderous roar. The huge and hideous dragon rose up from the lake with a snort of fire and prepared to strike, but George was too quick for him. With one well-aimed blow of his sword, he struck the dragon a fatal blow on his soft belly. The dragon reared backwards and crashed into the water with an almighty splash – dead.

George untied the princess and they rode back into the city to spread the good news. The king was so pleased that the dragon was dead, and so much more pleased that his daughter was safe, that he offered George the princess's hand in marriage. Soon, George and the princess were married and the whole of Silene came out to cheer.

BEOWULF'S LAST BATTLE

Beowulf was a hero and king who ruled over a Swedish tribe, the Geats, more than thirteen hundred years ago. In his youth, he gained fame and fortune by fighting and killing the evil monster, Grendel. In his old age, he fought his last and greatest battle against a fierce dragon. This is how it came about.

Beowulf had ruled the kingdom of the Geats for fifty years, wisely and justly. During that time, the kingdom had been at peace, its people safe and happy. However, as the saying goes, all good things have a nasty habit of coming to an end.

In Beowulf's kingdom, there lived a mighty, fire-breathing dragon who guarded a hoard of treasure hidden deep underground. No one knew where the dragon kept his treasure – no one dared go near to find out. Then one day a daring thief broke into the dragon's den, late at night, when the dragon was sleeping. Stacked from floor to ceiling were golden goblets, golden helmets and jewel-encrusted swords, all glimmering and glittering.

15

Now, the thief was not a wicked man. He was a poor slave who had run away from his master and was afraid to return in case he was beaten. Thinking that he could buy his way out of trouble with a small peace-offering, he picked up a golden cup and ran away as fast as he could.

'It's only a small cup,' he reassured himself, 'and there are so many – surely it won't be missed?'

How wrong can you be! The dragon had guarded this hoard of treasure for three hundred long years, and he knew every piece of it like the scales on the backs of his hands. As soon as he woke up, he knew something was wrong.

'Someone has been here,' he rumbled, in menace, 'I can smell their smell. And what is more . . . they have DARED to rob me of my treasure. They will be sorry, when I find them!'

The dragon was angrier than he had ever been. When night fell, he could hold back his fury no longer. He stormed out of his den and flew back and forth across the countryside, setting fire to houses and barns, and causing mayhem and terror wherever he went. Peace returned only when morning came and the dragon went back to his den for a rest. The people were frantic.

'What shall we do?' they cried. 'We can't fight the dragon and he is determined to destroy us. Oh, what shall we do?'

Beowulf, too, felt the full force of the dragon's wrath. The dragon set fire to the king's great hall and burned it to the ground. Beowulf was an old man now, with his best fighting days behind him. But he realised that it was his duty to save his people from a terrible fate. His trusty wooden shield would not last long against the dragon's fire, so he ordered a brand-new shield to be made from iron. Then he set off with eleven companions, and with the unfortunate thief who had caused the whole miserable mess as his guide.

When they reached the dragon's den, Beowulf turned to his companions and said: 'I have fought many battles in my time. Old as I am, to protect my people I shall fight again, and win. Go and wait for me in safety. This is a battle I must fight on my own.'

With these sombre words, he took up his sword and shiny, new shield and approached the entrance to the den.

'Come out and face me,' he cried to the dragon, 'and prepare to die!'

The ground began to shake and stir. Great clouds of fire and flame licked all around as Beowulf and the dragon came face to face. Beowulf raised his iron shield to block the fire and brought his ancient sword down with a crashing blow on the dragon's scales. But the sword simply bounced back off again, leaving not a mark on the dragon's back. The dragon hit back, engulfing Beowulf in a mass of licking flames that burned his hair and singed his grey beard.

Still Beowulf hacked away with his sword but after a few useless strokes the blade broke in his hands. As Beowulf reached for his sturdy dagger, the dragon sank his poisonous fangs into the king's neck. At that moment, Wiglaf, one of Beowulf's companions, rushed to the king's side. The other companions had taken fright and run away long ago.

'Watch out, my lord!' Wiglaf shouted. 'I will help all I can.'

Time and again Wiglaf stabbed his sword into the dragon's body, fired by fury and driven by courage. Together, the two warriors launched a savage attack from the cover of the iron shield and gradually, very gradually, the dragon's fire grew weaker until, finally, it went out.

Victory was theirs! The kingdom was saved. But for Beowulf, this was to be the last battle of his long life. The dragon's poison had spread through his body and he burned with a terrible fever. Beowulf fell to the scorched ground and took off his helmet. Through his pain he spoke, gasping for breath:

'You have acted like a son, Wiglaf, the son I never had. Take my helmet and my ring – you have earned them. Then go into the dragon's den and bring out some of the treasure hidden there, so that I can see it for myself once before I die.'

Wiglaf did as he was commanded.

'Thank you, Wiglaf,' whispered Beowulf. 'Now, one last thing. When I am dead, take my body and bury it on the cliffs, in view of the sea and the ships that sail on it.'

And with these words, Beowulf, king of the Geats, won his final battle but lost his life.

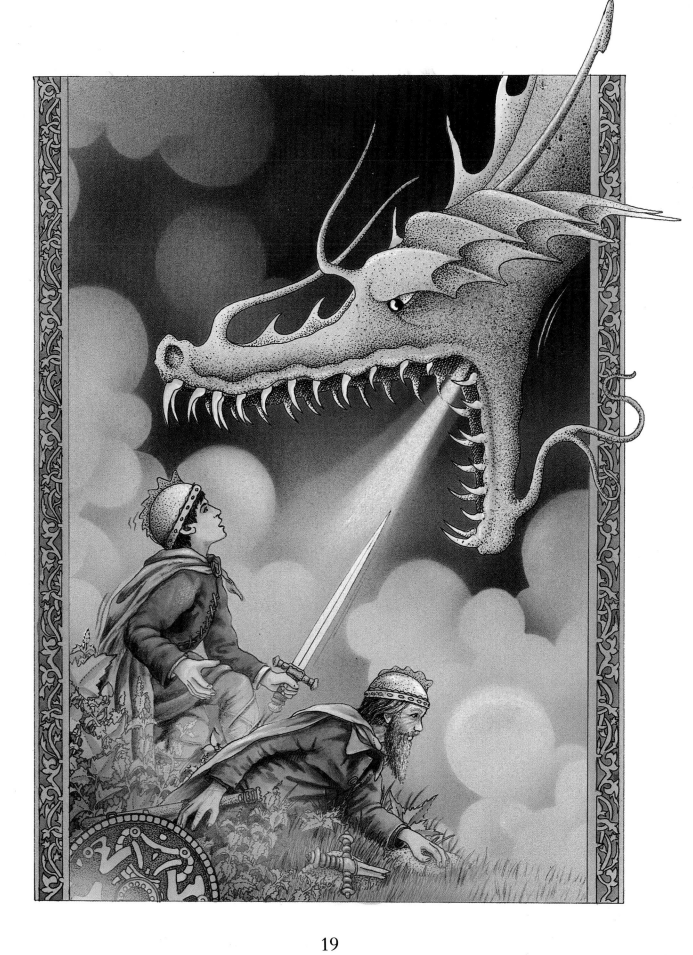

THE DRAGON UNDER THE MOUNTAIN

The story of the dragon under the mountain comes from Greece.

Long ago, there was a boy called Pepito who lived with his mother. Pepito earned his living chopping wood. One day, as he was working in the forest, he met a wealthy merchant.

'How would you like to earn some gold?' the merchant asked. 'All you need do is meet me at the harbour tomorrow and accompany me on a short sea voyage.'

'Done!' replied Pepito, without stopping to think.

Next day, with his mother's blessing, he set off for the harbour to meet the merchant. Six magnificent ships were ready to sail.

'Come with me,' the merchant said. 'I'll show you the ropes.'

Three days later, they reached an island which rose steep and black out of the sea. Its top was lost in cloud. Eagles soared and screeched around its cliffs. The ships dropped anchor.

'This is where you come in,' the merchant told Pepito. 'Climb to the top of the mountain and throw down anything you find there.'

'I can't climb that!' exclaimed Pepito. 'There's nothing to hold on . . .'

Before he could finish, a huge eagle swooped down, scooped him up and flew with him to the top of the mountain. Once he got his breath back, Pepito looked around. For as far as he could see, the ground was covered with lilies and roses. But these were no ordinary lilies and roses. Their leaves and petals sparkled with precious diamonds. Sapphires, rubies and emeralds glimmered and gleamed. Pepito couldn't believe his eyes. Then he remembered the merchant's orders and began to gather up handfuls of jewels and throw them down the mountainside. As fast as he threw, the sailors loaded the treasure into the ships, and then they sailed away . . .

Pepito shouted at the top of his voice.

'Hey! Hey! You can't leave me here! Come back! Come back!'

But the ships were already gone. Pepito threw himself down and banged his fists on the ground in dismay and despair.

'Stupid, stupid flowers!' he cried. 'Stupid, stupid jewels!'

Then he noticed a very strange thing. A hole had opened up in the ground, with a ladder leading down into the darkness. At the bottom of the ladder, a faint light burned. Pepito had no choice. He grabbed his sword and began slowly to climb down.

At the bottom of the ladder, a huge ruby lamp lit the way into a tunnel carved out of the rock. Pepito crawled along the tunnel and to his great astonishment found himself in a beautiful, sunny valley in which stood a fabulous marble palace. Pepito crept into the palace. There was no one about. In one room, he found a table laid with bread and butter and milk. He was very hungry now and so he tucked in. No sooner had he done so than a huge door at one end of the room flew open, and in flew a gigantic dragon with green wings, blue scales, gold horns, a golden tail, and silver talons on his feet. Pepito drew his sword.

He needn't have worried. The dragon was a kind but a very lonely dragon. He had lived on his own, under the mountain, for three thousand years. He was overjoyed to see Pepito.

'You will stay, won't you?' the dragon pleaded. 'Please say you'll stay.'

'Well, I can stay for a while,' replied Pepito, 'I suppose.'

'Oh, thank you. Thank you,' said the dragon. 'You don't know what it's been like, with no father and no mother, and no friends or relations . . .'

So Pepito stayed with the dragon and the dragon waited on Pepito hand and foot, in case the boy changed his mind and went away. Soon, Pepito began to forget about his mother and his home. He and the dragon were all set to live happily ever after. Until one day, in a far corner of the palace, Pepito stumbled upon a little door that he had never seen before.

'Where does that door lead?' he asked the dragon.

'Oh, please don't make me tell you!' the dragon replied.

This only made Pepito keener to know, and eventually the dragon gave him a golden key and told him to see for himself. Pepito unlocked the door and stepped through into a beautiful garden, full of flowers.

'It's very lovely,' he told the dragon. 'But I don't quite know what all the fuss is about.'

Just then, a pink pigeon flew into the garden. It fluttered down to the edge of the garden pond and turned into a beautiful girl in a flowing feather dress. The girl stepped into the pond and began to bathe. Pepito fell in love there and then, at first sight. He begged the girl to stay but she turned back into a pigeon and flew away.

'How can I see her again?' Pepito asked the dragon.

'I'd be careful, if I was you,' said the dragon, rather ungraciously. 'For one thing, it's pretty stupid to fall in love with a pigeon. And for another thing, her father's a magician and her mother's a witch. They turned her into a pigeon as punishment. So there!'

But Pepito would not be put off. He went on and on about it, and finally the dragon gave in.

'If you really want her to stay,' he said crossly, 'wait till she comes to bathe again, then steal her feather dress. She can't fly away without her feathers . . . But don't say I didn't warn you,' he muttered, under his breath.

Next day, Pepito hid in the garden, waiting for the pigeon girl to return to the pond. Then, while she was bathing, Pepito ran out of his hiding place and stole her feather dress.

'Now you'll have to stay,' he told her, 'and do me the honour of becoming my wife.'

'I accept,' said the girl.

And that was that. The dragon sulked for several days when he heard the news. But he cheered up by and by and gave the girl a fine wedding dress and even conducted the wedding ceremony in great, grand style. He warned Pepito to burn the feather dress but Pepito decided to keep it, for it was too beautiful to burn.

Pepito and his wife had two children and for a very long time they all lived happily with the dragon. One night, however, Pepito dreamed of his mother's home and longed to see her again.

'If you really want to go,' said the dragon, sadly. 'I can't stop you.'

He gave Pepito a bag of gold and made him promise to come back as soon as he could.

'Now turn round, close your eyes, and think of home,' he said.

When Pepito opened his eyes again, there he was at his mother's house, with his wife and two children, enjoying a tearful reunion. With his bag of dragon gold, Pepito bought a farm. The family prospered and the memory of the dragon faded away.

One day, when Pepito's wife was spring-cleaning their house, she came across her old feather dress. She stroked it gently and gave both her children a feather each. At once, all three turned into pigeons and flew away.

'Pepito, Pepito!' she called through the air. 'Look for us by the five white towers.'

Beside himself with grief, Pepito began his search at once. First he visited the dragon. The dragon was delighted to see his old friend after so long, but his face quickly fell when he heard Pepito's story.

'I told you so,' he said, sulkily.

But being a kindly soul, the dragon once again agreed to help. He gave Pepito a hat to make him invisible, a rusty magic sword and a branch of a tree to ride on. Pepito put on the hat and sat on the branch of the tree.

'Take me to the five white towers!' he commanded, and off he flew, leaving the dragon more lonely than ever.

The tree branch carried Pepito to a tall white mountain where five tall, white marble towers soared into the sky. Pepito ran from tower to tower, calling and calling. No one called back. At last he stumbled into a little yard behind the fifth tower, and sitting there was his wife, dressed in rags. Pepito took off his hat to make himself visible, and his wife ran into his arms. But before they could plot their escape, the door of the tower flew open with an icy cold blast. It was the girl's father – the dreaded magician.

'I can smell a man!' he roared. 'Where are you, you miserable creature?'

Pepito meanwhile had pulled on his hat so he couldn't be seen. This made the magician crosser than ever. He ranted and raged, and stamped his feet.

'Father, please,' said the girl. 'It's only my husband come to find me. Please let us go.'

'Hah!' scoffed the magician. 'Let him prove himself first. If he can knock down this mountain and transform it into a beautiful garden, he can have you. But he's only got till tomorrow morning! Hah! hah! hah!'

However, the magician didn't know about Pepito's magic sword. The sword turned into a pick and hacked away at the hard rock. In no time at all it had flattened the mountain. Then it turned into a spade and dug the soil to make a garden. By the following morning, the garden was full of the most beautiful flowers ever seen.

The magician turned positively purple with rage. He and his wife, the witch, rode out of the tower on the back of a dragoness and chased after Pepito. Then the magic sword turned into an axe. It chopped off the magician's head and the witch's head with two mighty blows. Pepito, his wife and their children climbed aboard the tree branch, ready to go home. They also took the dragoness with them and introduced her to the dragon under the mountain, so that he need never be lonely again.

SEAN, DRAGON SLAYER

This story is a tale from Ireland which, in ancient times, was known as Erin.

The king of Erin had thirteen sons. One day, a wise man advised him to give one of his sons to Fate, to ensure peace and happiness for himself and his kingdom. The king drew lots and pulled out the name of his thirteenth son, Sean. He gave Sean a horse and a sword, and sent him on his way.

Sean rode for many miles, until he came to a land where three mighty giants lived in three mighty castles. When the first giant saw Sean, he smiled and licked his lips.

'He looks nice and tasty,' the giant chuckled. 'And I'm HUNGRY!' But before the giant could open his mouth to take a bite, Sean drew out his sword and killed him.

The second giant had the same idea. So did the third. But Sean killed both of them with two blows of his sword. Then he took a black horse from the first castle, a brown horse from the second castle and a red horse from the third castle, where he also found a pair of blue glass boots. He disguised himself as a cowherd, so that no one would guess his true identity, and went to work for king of that land.

In the sea nearby, there lived a fearsome dragon. This dragon had an enormous mouth with swords for fangs. Every seven years, the dragon was given a young girl for his dinner. This year's unfortunate victim was none other than the daughter of the king. The king sent out a challenge. Whoever could slay the dragon and save his daughter, could have her hand in marriage. Hundreds of champions came from far and wide to try their luck. But at the first sight of the dragon and his jagged jaws, they all turned tail and fled.

Then Sean rode by on the fine black horse. He saw the princess sitting on the shore, waiting to be eaten. As the dragon came out of the sea, Sean drew his sword and cut off the dragon's head. But the head flew back on to the dragon's body and the dragon plunged back into the sea.

'I'll be back,' he hissed.

Sean went back to his cows and the princess went back to the palace.

Next day, the princess went and sat all by herself on the seashore. All the champions had given up and gone home by now. Nothing could save her.

Then Sean came riding by on the fine brown horse. As the dragon came out of the sea, Sean drew his sword and cut the dragon's body clean in two. But the two halves joined back together again and the dragon rushed back into the sea.

'You'll have to try harder than that,' he chortled. 'I'll be back tomorrow!'

So the princess went back to the palace and Sean went back to his cows. He needed to think.

'How can I kill this dragon once and for all?' he puzzled. 'I can't go on fighting him every day for the rest of my life.'

Then he had an idea. He galloped off to the third giant's castle to see the wise old woman who lived in one of the towers. She was grateful to Sean for saving her from the giant and giving her a home.

'Put your sword away,' she told him. 'It's no use against a dragon. Take this wizened old apple instead. Put it in the dragon's mouth and then see what happens.'

Next day, Sean came riding by the shore again, this time on the fine red horse and wearing the pair of blue glass boots. The princess was sitting all by herself. As the dragon reared out of the water and opened his mouth to roar, Sean threw in the apple, quick as a flash. The dragon fell on to the shore. His huge body sizzled and started to melt. Soon, all that remained of him was a pool of brown jelly which the waves washed out to sea.

The princess jumped to her feet and ran to thank Sean. But he had turned his horse and was galloping away. All the princess could catch hold of was one of Sean's blue glass boots.

There was great rejoicing at the news that the dragon was dead. The king joyfully proclaimed his daughter's forthcoming marriage to the Dragon Slayer. But who was the Dragon Slayer and, more importantly, where was he? The only evidence of his existence was one blue glass boot.

The king ordered all the unmarried men in his kingdom to come forward and try the boot on. But the boot didn't fit anyone. Hundreds of young men went away disappointed. The king was at his wits' end. He sent for the wisest man at the court to give him some advice.

'Find the cowherd who killed the three giants,' the wise man told the king. 'He's your man.'

The king sent a band of strong men to find the giant-killer. The men visited each castle in turn, and found Sean eating his supper in the third castle. Sean had no desire to go to the palace. He tied the men up and dumped them in the cellar. Then he went on with his supper.

The king sent out some more men but Sean tied them up too, and dumped them with the others in the cellar. The king decided that there was nothing for it – he would have to go and fetch Sean himself. He went to the first castle, then to the second castle, then to the third castle, where he found Sean.

'You must come to my palace and try on the blue glass boot,' the king said. 'You're my last hope. It doesn't fit anybody else.'

At first, Sean refused, politely but firmly. The king pleaded and begged and finally burst into tears. This was more than Sean could bear. He went back to the palace and tried on the blue glass boot. And, of course, it was a perfect fit.

'I'd be honoured to marry the princess,' Sean said. 'And she can feel proud to marry me, for my father is the king of Erin, and I am a prince not a cowherd.'

So Prince Sean and the princess were married and went to live in the third giant's castle. And, as far as we know, they did indeed live happily ever after.

THE GIANT WITH THE TEETH OF FIRE

This giant story comes from the Fiji Islands, which lie in the Pacific Ocean to the north of New Zealand.

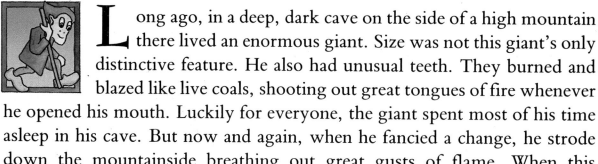

Long ago, in a deep, dark cave on the side of a high mountain there lived an enormous giant. Size was not this giant's only distinctive feature. He also had unusual teeth. They burned and blazed like live coals, shooting out great tongues of fire whenever he opened his mouth. Luckily for everyone, the giant spent most of his time asleep in his cave. But now and again, when he fancied a change, he strode down the mountainside breathing out great gusts of flame. When this happened, all the people in the nearby villages left their homes and ran for their lives.

The young men who lived near the mountain were jealous of the fire coming from the giant's teeth. For the people of the islands had not yet discovered how to make fire for themselves.

'Just think what we could do if we had the giant's fire!' they said. 'We could eat roasted fish and baked vegetables. We could have light and heat even on the darkest, coldest nights.'

So some of the bravest young men decided to steal the giant's fire. Armed with bundles of dried leaves and twigs, they crept up the mountain to the giant's cave and peeked inside. The giant was fast asleep, and snoring. With each snore, a blast of fire shot out of his mouth and lit up the whole cave. Treading very carefully, the young men crept closer and closer to the giant, until they were near enough to light their bundles of twigs and leaves from the spluttering flames around his mouth. Then they turned and started to tiptoe away, out of the cave to safety.

30

Just as the last young man was creeping out of the cave, his bundle of twigs brushed against the giant's cheek. The giant sat up, wide awake. He soon noticed the line of light sneaking its way down the mountainside.

'Woe betide those who have stolen my fire,' he roared. 'When I catch up with them, I'll roast them and eat them!'

And he stomped down the mountain in search of the thieves.

The young men raced down the mountainside, with the giant's footsteps pounding in their ears. At the foot of the mountain, they found a small cave. Quickly, they all jumped in and rolled a large stone across the entrance to keep the giant out. Then they lit a fire, and waited.

The giant reached the cave and tried to shift the stone. He pushed and shoved but the stone would not move. Then he had an idea.

'Alright, you win, I give up,' he said, in the gentlest voice he could manage. 'If you let me in, we can all be friends.'

The young men did not trust the giant to be friends with anyone – but it was getting rather stuffy inside the cave.

'Let's move the stone just a little bit,' one of them said. 'That will keep the giant happy and let in some air.'

They moved the stone to make a small gap but the giant was not in the least satisfied with that.

'I can't even get my head inside,' he said. 'How can we be friends if I can't see what you look like?'

The giant wanted to get his head inside the cave so that he could breathe fire and burn the young men to cinders. The young men guessed his thoughts.

'Very well,' they said. 'Put your head up close to the stone so that you can see inside when we roll it away.'

And then they pushed. But they did not roll the stone away. Instead, they shoved it straight at the giant's head and knocked him dead. His teeth of fire grew dark and cold, and finally went out altogether.

A great feast was held to celebrate the giant's death, and for the first time the people of the island tasted delicious roasted fish and baked vegetables, and danced around a roaring, blazing fire.

BABA YAGA
COUNTS THE SPOONS

The wicked witch, Baba Yaga, is a popular character in many eastern European folktales. This story comes from Russia.

A sparrow, a cat and a brave boy lived together in a hut in a forest. One day, they ran short of wood for the fire, and the cat and the sparrow went out to cut some more.

'A word of warning,' they said to the boy before they left. 'If Baba Yaga comes to count the spoons, keep very quiet, or she'll eat you.'

'Right ho!' replied the boy, and settled down for a nap by the fire.

A little while later, the door flew open. Baba Yaga came into the hut and started to count the spoons.

'This is the sparrow's spoon, and this is the cat's spoon, and this is the spoon of the brave boy,' she said.

The boy opened his eyes. He was so cross when he saw Baba Yaga looking at his spoon that he completely forgot his friends' advice.

'Baba Yaga, put my spoon down,' he shouted. He was brave indeed, if rather hasty.

Then Baba Yaga grabbed hold of the boy's hair, and raced out of the hut on her pestle and mortar.

'Friend cat! Friend sparrow!' the boy cried. 'Save me! Save me!'

The cat came running and the sparrow came flying. One scratched, one pecked at Baba Yaga until she let the boy go.

The next day, the sparrow and the cat set out again to chop more firewood.

'Today we are going further afield,' they told the boy. 'So don't cause any more trouble with Baba Yaga. We might not hear your call for help.'

'Right ho!' the boy replied, and settled down for a nap by the fire.

Soon the door flew open and in stomped Baba Yaga to count the spoons.

'This is the sparrow's spoon, and this is the cat's spoon, and this is the spoon of that brave boy,' she crooned.

The boy tried to bite his tongue, but the sight of Baba Yaga drooling over his spoon was just too much for him to bear.

'Baba Yaga, put my spoon down!' he cried.

Once again, Baba Yaga grabbed the boy by his hair and dragged him out.

'Friend sparrow! Friend cat!' the boy shrieked. 'Save me! Save me!'

The cat and the sparrow were just within earshot, and both hurried quickly back. One scratched, one pecked at Baba Yaga until she let the boy go.

On the third day, the cat and the sparrow set out again into the forest.

'Today we are going far away,' they told the boy. 'And if you call, we won't be able to hear you. So stay out of trouble!'

'Right ho!' replied the boy, from his perch by the fire.

He dozed for an hour or so, thinking himself safe. But soon, sure enough, Baba Yaga appeared and began once again to count all the spoons.

'This is the cat's spoon, and this is the sparrow's spoon and this is the spoon of the brave boy,' she cackled. 'And a very nice spoon it is, too. I think I shall keep it!'

At this, the boy could keep quiet no longer.

'For the very last time, Baba Yaga,' he cried. 'Put my spoon down!'

And, for the very last time, Baba Yaga grabbed the boy by his hair, and set off through the forest. This time no one heard his cries for help.

Baba Yaga took the boy back to her hut, deep in the forest. She locked him in the wood shed and said to her first daughter,

'Cook this boy for my dinner. I'll be back to eat him!' And off she flew.

The first daughter stoked the fire and heated up the oven. Then she fetched the boy and told him to lie in the roasting pan.

'Like this?' he said, with his feet on the floor and his head in the pan.

'No, not like that!' the daughter said. 'Like this!' And she showed him.

Quick as a flash, the boy picked up the roasting pan and popped it into the oven, daughter and all. Then he waited for Baba Yaga to return. She was licking her lips at the thought of her dinner.

'I hope you like the taste of roast daughter,' the boy called.

Baba Yaga was furious. She summoned her second daughter and ordered her to cook the boy. Then she went out.

So the second daughter stoked the fire and heated up the oven. She fetched the boy and ordered him to lie in the roasting pan.

'Like this?' he enquired, with one leg in the tray and one leg outside.

'No, not like that!' the daughter replied. 'Like this, stupid!' And she showed him. Into the oven she was popped, in no time at all, just like her elder sister.

The third daughter tried, and the third daughter failed. Baba Yaga was beside herself with rage.

'This has gone far enough!' she fumed. 'I shall just have to roast the brave boy myself!'

She fetched him from the wood shed and told him to lie down in the roasting pan.

'Like this?' he asked, with his feet in the tray and his head on the ground.

'No, not like that, you imbecile!' Baba Yaga screeched. 'Like this!' And she sat in the pan, ready for roasting. The boy popped her straight into the oven, just like her daughters. Then he ran all the way home and told the cat and the sparrow how he had outwitted the witch and saved their spoons.

THE DWARF AND THE SALT GRINDER

This is a story which gives an explanation of why the sea is salty.
It comes from ancient China.

 Long ago, two brothers, Ah Bong and Ah Dong, lived in China by the sea. Ah Bong was greedy and lazy. Ah Dong was generous and hard-working. Ah Bong spent all day lazing about at home. Ah Dong worked for his living all day and cooked and cleaned all night.

One day, as usual, Ah Dong left home early in the morning to chop firewood. He took a bowl of rice for his lunch. But as he lifted his axe, a scrawny old dwarf leapt out from behind the tree.

'Kind sir,' he said, in a thin, pleading voice. 'Can you spare some food? I've not eaten a proper meal for weeks.'

Ah Dong felt sorry for the hungry dwarf and gave him half of his lunch. The dwarf grabbed the rice and gobbled it down. Then he looked longingly at the other half until Ah Dong gave in and let him eat that, too.

'Thank you, thank you,' the dwarf said, happily. 'You are a very good man to part with your lunch. And one good turn deserves another.'

He took out an old stone box and lifted out a small stone grinder. He gave it to Ah Dong.

'This is a magic grinder,' he told Ah Dong. 'It will grind whatever you want it to. And when you want it to stop, you just have to ask it. But don't forget to say "Please"!'

The dwarf departed and Ah Dong returned to his work. By lunchtime, he was very hungry. He turned to the grinder for help.

'Grind me some rice,' he commanded.

At once, the grinder set to work, producing bowl after bowl of delicious smelling rice.

'Please stop!' said Ah Dong, after a while. And it stopped. The rice tasted as good as it smelt. Ah Dong ate a good bowlful, then took the rest home, with his axe and his grinder.

As soon as Ah Bong caught the smell of the rice, he leapt out of bed and began to tuck in. Ah Dong told him about the dwarf and the grinder. Then Ah Dong set the grinder down in the kitchen and ordered it to produce some dinner. Dish after mouth-watering dish appeared, until Ah Dong asked it politely to stop.

Ah Dong had lots of good ideas about how to use the grinder wisely and well. But his brother would have none of it.

'We should use the grinder to get rich,' he said. 'That's what we should do. We'll tell it to grind the finest salt. Then we'll sell it and make both our fortunes.'

Ah Dong suggested they wait until morning before making their minds up, and off he went to bed. But Ah Bong had other ideas. That night, he took the grinder and sneaked out of the house and down to the harbour. He boarded a ship and sailed away, as far from his brother as he could go. When the ship reached the open sea, Ah Bong put his plan into action. He took out the grinder, set it on the deck and ordered it to start grinding salt. It ground and ground and, as it ground, Ah Bong shovelled the salt into sacks.

But the salt came faster than Ah Bong could shovel, and soon it reached up to his ankles and began to creep along the deck. Time after time, he ordered the grinder to stop but it took no notice and carried on. After all, Ah Bong had not asked it properly. He had forgotten to say 'Please'!

Great piles of salt poured out of the grinder. Soon it came up to Ah Bong's knees and covered the deck. The ship's captain and crew begged Ah Bong to stop the grinder, for the ship would surely sink if it did not stop. They tried to sweep the salt overboard. It didn't work. Some of the crew even jumped from the ship and tried to swim for the shore. In no time at all, Ah Bong was the only one left. Still the grinder went on grinding until the salt reached Ah Bong's neck and swamped the entire ship. Finally, the ship sank beneath the waves, and Ah Bong was drowned. But no one asked the grinder to stop and it grinds on still, and that is why the sea is salty.

THE SHRINKING GIANTS

The story of how the giants were brought down to size
is another tale from ancient China.

Many thousands of years ago, the gods made their home on a group of five islands in the middle of the sea. They lived there peacefully and contentedly, in palaces built out of precious jade. The only things to disturb their carefree lives were the terrible storms that struck from time to time, rocking and tossing the islands, and scattering them across the sea. When this happened, the gods had to fly to heaven and wait there for the storm to pass.

After one particularly violent storm, the gods decided that something must be done. They begged the god of the sea to find a way of fixing their islands firmly to the sea bed. So the sea god set off in search of help. He found it in the shape of the five giant tortoises that guarded his underwater palace.

'Each of you must tie an island to your back,' he ordered the tortoises, 'and stand your ground.'

For many years, the gods were more than happy with this arrangement. No matter how strong the storms, their islands stood solid and firm. But then a series of earthquakes began to shake the islands. The gods asked the sea god what was wrong.

'It's like this,' the sea god told them. 'The tortoises need some exercise. So they get restless and start moving around. I'll tell them to leave the islands once a year and have a good long swim. That should solve the problem.'

And for many years, it did.

Now, a family of giants lived on the far side of one of the islands. They were so tall that their heads brushed the clouds and with each giant stride they could cover a hundred miles or more. They lived quite happily alongside the gods.

One day, the youngest giant decided to go on a fishing trip. He sat on a cliff-top and waited. All morning he sat there and caught not a thing. Then he spied the tortoises having their yearly swim.

'What a good catch a tortoise would be,' he thought to himself. So he baited his line with chunks of fresh fish and cast it into the sea. The tortoises were always hungry and, one by one, they took the bait. The giant hauled all five tortoises out of the sea and on to the cliff.

That night, the islands were hit by an almighty storm. The storm was so violent that two of the islands were tossed to the North Pole and two to the South Pole. The other island sank to the bottom of the sea. The gods were furious. They cursed the youngest giant for his thoughtlessness and cursed the tortoises for their greed. They decided to punish all the giants.

'We'll shrink every giant in the land,' they vowed. 'We'll shrink them to the size of trees.'

And this is how the giants stayed, from that day and for evermore.

The tortoises were punished, too. After years of searching far and wide, the sea god managed to find the five islands and bring them back. He tied each tortoise to an island and forbade any of them ever to move again.

HOW FINN FOUND BRAN

In Irish legends, Finn MacCool is a great hero and warrior. He was very tall and strong – almost a giant himself. This is the story of how he fought a giant and found his faithful hunting-dog, Bran.

 In a rare lull between battles, the mighty Finn MacCool went for a walk, all by himself. He wanted to think. But he hadn't gone far when he met a man he had never seen before.

'Who are you?' asked Finn MacCool.

'I'm a clever man, looking for work. My talent is that I never sleep,' replied the man.

'You can work for me,' Finn said.

A few miles on, he met another stranger.

'I'm a clever man, looking for work,' this stranger told him. 'My talent is that I can hear the softest sound, even the grass growing from the ground.'

'Then come with me,' said Finn. 'I'm sure I could use your skills.'

There was another stranger, a few miles on.

'I'm a clever man, looking for work,' he said. 'My talent is my strength. I'm the strongest man in the world.'

'Then I'll take you on,' said Finn.

And so it went on. Finn met four more strangers on his walk, all looking for work. He invited them all to go with him. One was a master thief; one could climb like a cat; another threw stones that turned into walls, and the fourth was an expert marksman.

Later that evening, Finn found himself at the gates of a palace he had never seen before. In the palace lived a king and queen, and they were in despair.

'Demons and devils stole our first two children, and we're afraid they'll take our new baby, too,' they told Finn.

'I will help you, if I can,' said Finn. 'My new band of workers will guard your baby.'

He told the man who never slept to guard the baby in its nursery. He told the man who could hear the grass grow to sit by the door and listen for intruders. The world's strongest man sat by the baby's cradle, ready to grab anyone who came near.

Just before midnight, the man who could hear the grass grow heard the faintest sound of music. It was getting nearer, and he was beginning to feel very sleepy.

'Oh no!' the other guards moaned. 'It's fairy music. It will put us all to sleep. Then who will guard the baby?'

'Nonsense!' said the man who never slept. He went round the guards shaking them in turn and waking them up whenever they dropped off. Suddenly, the world's strongest man saw a long, hairy arm come through the nursery window and try to snatch the baby. He grabbed the arm and pulled and pulled until, finally, he pulled the arm right off. But in all the excitement he didn't notice the other arm that sneaked silently through the window and stole the baby.

Finn swore an oath to the king and queen that he and his men would find the baby, whatever it took. He asked for a boat and they sailed away, until they reached a lonely beach on which a single, solitary house was built. The walls of the house were sheer and slippery.

'Climb to the top of the house,' Finn told the expert climber. 'Look down the chimney and tell me what you see.'

The climber was at the top of the house in a trice. Down the chimney he could see a one-eyed, one-armed giant holding a baby in his hand, with two little boys by his feet.

'Now it's your turn,' Finn instructed the master thief. 'Go into the house and steal back the three children.'

Quiet as a mouse, the thief crept into the giant's house and stole the children right from under his nose. As he turned to go, he noticed three puppies playing on the floor. So he stole them, too, and took them back to Finn. Then they all set off back to the boat. They hadn't gone far when they heard barking behind them. An enormous brown dog was bounding towards them. The mother dog had come to rescue her puppies. The man who threw stones that turned into walls threw stone after stone. But the enormous brown dog simply leapt straight over them.

'Leave the puppies for her,' said Finn. So they left one of the puppies, then another. Finally, they reached their boat and began to row for home.

Just before they reached the shore, the sea began to bubble and boil. The giant rose up from the lashing waves, his one eye blazing with fury.

'Leave him to me,' said the marksman.

He put an arrow in his bow and fired straight into the giant's eye. The giant toppled back into the sea with a terrible crash. He was never seen again.

The king and queen were overjoyed to see their children safe and sound.

'How can we reward you?' they asked Finn.

'I don't want a reward,' he smiled. 'But I'll keep this puppy and take him home. And I'll call him Bran.'

So Finn found Bran. From then on wherever Finn went, Bran went too, and vice versa. For Bran was no ordinary dog. He had a magic claw that could cause a wound which would never heal. When Finn's enemies caught sight of Bran, they fled for their lives, without stopping to fight.

STORMALONG AND THE KRAKEN

Sailors crossing the North Atlantic Ocean were terrified by stories of a giant sea monster called the kraken. Few people who had seen the kraken lived to tell the tale. Among the lucky survivors was an American sea captain, Alfred Bulltop Stormalong.

Captain Stormalong had made his mind up.
'I'm giving up the sea,' he declared.
After all, in his long career, he had sailed round the world and back again and it was high time for a rest. But when he was asked to take command of a brand-new ship, called the *Tuscarora*, he just couldn't say no. His first, fateful voyage aboard the *Tuscarora* was to Sweden, to collect a cargo of pickled fish.

Stormalong plotted the route carefully. He decided to sail through the Kattegat, a narrow channel of sea between Denmark and Sweden. Some of the crew were less than happy when they heard this news.

'But Captain,' one sailor said, 'that's where the kraken lives.'

The kraken was the most terrifying of all sea monsters, a hideous creature with the body of an octopus and a writhing trail of tentacles. Many a ship and many a crew had been dragged underwater and drowned by the kraken.

But Stormalong told his crew. 'The kraken doesn't frighten me. I've seen far worse, I can tell you.' And he set course for Stockholm.

At first, all went well. But as the ship turned into the Kattegat, the sailors' fears were realised. The sea began to swirl and froth. Great black spinning whirlpools opened up before the ship, threatening to suck it down into the murky depths. The sailors cowered below deck and trembled with fear.

'It's the kraken,' they moaned. 'We'll all be drowned!'

But Captain Stormalong was not beaten yet. He kept his hands firmly on the wheel and racked his brains.

'All hands on deck!' he shouted, as an idea struck him. 'Hoist the sails!'

The sailors set to work. The *Tuscarora* sped through the water, then, on a sudden squally gust of wind, took to the air and flew right over the kraken's head. By early next morning, the ship had reached the port of Stockholm, safe and sound. The sailors spent a happy evening in the town, bragging about how they'd bravely outwitted the kraken. Captain Stormalong wisely kept his thoughts to himself.

Next morning, captain and crew loaded their cargo of pickled fish. Soon the ship passed once more into the narrow channel of the Kattegat.

Before very long, the kraken reared its ugly head once again. The water whirled and roared; the ship tossed to and fro. Captain Stormalong held the wheel firmly and prepared to follow the same plan as before. But just at that moment the wind began to drop. Soon it had died away completely. The ship was stranded within the kraken's reach.

Stormalong had to think quickly. He blamed himself for getting his ship and crew into such peril. He stared at the sea and consulted his charts. There was only one thing to do.

'Bring me the biggest harpoon we've got,' he told the first mate.

Stormalong prepared to strike. He waited, his eyes fixed on the sea ahead.

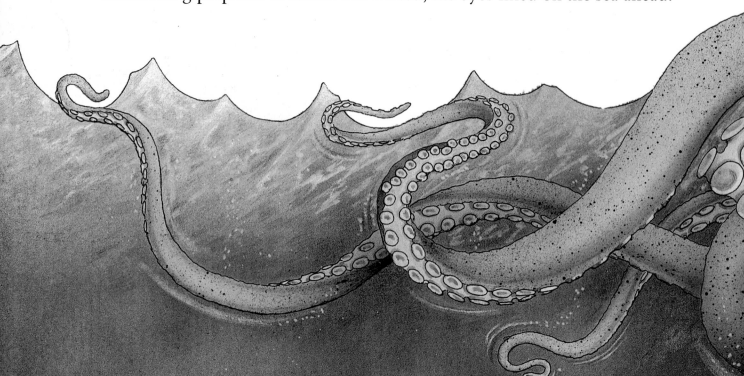

Just then the kraken raised its fearful head above
the waves and looked straight at Stormalong.

Stormalong fired. The harpoon flew through the air
and pierced the kraken's neck. The monster lashed out
with its tentacles, and writhed in agony. In a desperate
dive, it plunged back into the water and under the ship.
It was all the crew could do to keep the ship upright as
the dying kraken turned this way and that. Finally,
the kraken sank to the depths of the sea, dead.

The wind began to blow and the *Tuscarora*'s sails
began to billow. The sailors cheered.

'We're saved, we're saved,' they sang.

And this is how Stormalong killed the kraken and
saved the day – although it was a very close thing.

THE RAINBOW SERPENT

In the myths of the Australian Aborigines, snakes are powerful, magical creatures that live in waterholes, deep underground. This is a story about the rainbow serpent.

 ong ago, there was a time called Dreamtime. This was the time when the land was flat and featureless. There were no lakes or rivers or valleys or hills. There was just the sky, the sun and the rain. That was all.

One day, after a shower of rain, a brilliant rainbow appeared in the sky. It turned into a mighty serpent and slithered down to earth.

'I must find my people,' the rainbow serpent said. 'People who speak my own language.'

And off he slithered across the countryside, grinding out valleys and pushing up mountains as he went. Each time he saw the flames of a camp fire, he crept as close as he dared and listened. But he never understood what the people were saying.

The going got tougher and the land got harder. The rainbow serpent no longer had the strength or will to carve out valleys with his scales. Then, one day, he heard the sound of people singing and at long last he understood the words. The people were dancing around their camp fire. The rainbow serpent slithered towards them.

'I am the rainbow serpent,' he said. 'And you are my people.'

The people welcomed the rainbow serpent and he lived in their camp with them. He taught them more dances and songs, and showed them how to paint their bodies and how to make necklaces out of feathers and bones. Everyone was happy and contented. And so a whole year passed.

One day, the sky grew dark and filled with great black rain clouds. The people built huts for shelter. But as the rain began two boys came running into the camp, returning from a hunting trip. There was no time for them to build a hut, and it was now raining very hard.

'Please give us shelter!' they cried. But no one would.

'Please let us share some shelter!' they pleaded. But no one would.

The rainbow serpent, who had been fast asleep, opened wide his great mouth and said to the boys, 'You can come in here. There's plenty of room.'

So the boys ran into the rainbow serpent's mouth, and the rainbow serpent swallowed them whole.

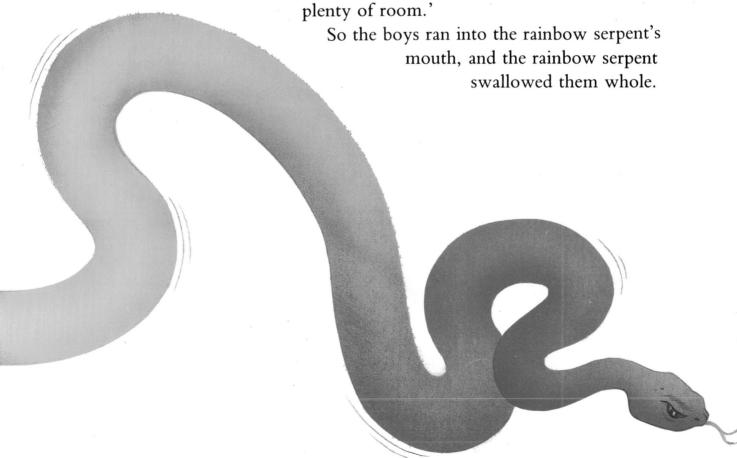

When the rainbow serpent thought about what he had done, he felt truly ashamed of himself.

'I'll be driven out of the camp,' he thought. 'The people won't want me here any more.'

That night he crept sadly out of the camp and travelled far away.

Next morning, the people looked high and low for the rainbow serpent and for the two missing boys but they were nowhere to be found.

'Did they shelter in your hut?' everyone was asked.

'No, there wasn't enough room,' they all replied.

Then the awful truth dawned on them.

'The rainbow serpent must have eaten them,' the head man said. 'Let's go after him and find out.'

So the men picked up their hunting spears and set off in search of the rainbow serpent. His tracks were easy to follow and soon they found him coiled around a mountaintop, fast asleep. The men crept up to the rainbow serpent as quietly as night, slit open his side with their knives, and released the two boys he had swallowed. But the two boys had turned into parrots with feathers all the colours of the rainbow, and they flew away.

'At least they are free now,' the men said to each other. Then they climbed down the mountain and started for home. Just as they reached the bottom of the mountain, the men heard something stirring on the slopes above them. It was the rainbow serpent – and he was furious.

'How dare you do such a thing to me?' he hissed. 'You'll be sorry, I'll make sure of that.'

Then he coiled his coils around the mountain, tighter and tighter, until the mountain broke under the strain. Boulders and rocks rained down on the men below and great lumps of mountain went flying all over the countryside to make the small hills you see today.

The men were terrified. The serpent hissed and spat, and flicked its forked tongue in and out of its mouth. Some men turned tail and ran for their lives. Others turned into animals and hid underground. Tighter and tighter the serpent wound his coils. The sky flashed with lightning. Thunder boomed and roared. The mountain was flattened to the ground. Then the rainbow serpent, exhausted by his efforts, slid away to a deep waterhole where he lives to this day. The land he left behind was never the same again. For now there were lakes and rivers and hills.

The men went back to their home and told their story by the camp fire. They never saw the rainbow serpent again – that is, except after a shower of rain. Then he often appeared as a brilliant rainbow to light the sky.

THE DAY THAT THOR WENT FISHING

In Viking mythology, the Earth was surrounded by a vast ocean and in the ocean lived a gigantic serpent, Jormungand. His snaky body was so long it completely encircled the Earth with room to spare. This is the story of what happened to Jormungand when Thor, the thunder god, went fishing.

Armed with his trusty hammer, Mjolnir, Thor had many daring adventures. He fought giants and monsters galore, but his burning ambition was to fight and kill the terrible serpent, Jormungand. For every time Jormungand stirred, his coils whipped up the wind and stirred up the waves, causing violent storms and tempests.

Disguised as a young warrior, Thor set off for a distant land by the sea. There he met the giant, Hymir, and asked him for shelter. Next day, he begged the giant to take him fishing. Hymir agreed, unwillingly.

'You can come on one condition,' he grumbled. 'That you do what I tell you and you don't get in the way.'

'I'll do whatever you say,' Thor replied. 'Now, tell me, what sort of bait do I need?'

'Oh well, if you don't even know that,' said Hymir, rudely, 'why should I tell you?' And off he stomped.

Thor was getting angry now and was tempted to teach the giant a lesson he wouldn't forget. Instead, he went to the giant's herd of bulls, killed the biggest bull, cut off its head and tossed it into the boat as bait. Then he grabbed the oars and began to row. Even Hymir had to admit that Thor was a far better rower than he. Thor rowed faster and faster until they were well beyond the giant's usual fishing grounds and close to the place where the great serpent lay.

Hymir cast his line and after a while caught two huge whales. He was very smug and pleased with himself.

'You'll never beat that!' he boasted to Thor.

Thor cast his line, baited with the bull's head, into the sea. Immediately, the serpent lunged at the bait and gobbled it greedily down. The serpent thrashed to and fro in the water as the hook caught its throat and Thor struggled to haul him in. The boat rocked and swayed and almost capsized, but Thor braced himself against the sides and heaved and pulled with all his strength. Finally, with a mighty shout and a mighty splash, he landed the serpent in the boat.

The serpent lay in the bottom of the boat, its enormous coils writhing and wriggling, spitting venom from its hideous mouth. The giant, Hymir, was scared out of his wits and begged Thor to let the serpent go. But Thor lifted his hammer and prepared to bring down a fatal blow on the serpent's head. Just as he raised his arm, Hymir leaped forward in panic, cut the fishing line with his knife and let the serpent slither and slide back into the sea. Quick as a flash, Thor threw his hammer after the serpent, hitting him right between the eyes. Dazed and stunned, Jormungand sank to the depths of the sea and died, never to be seen or heard of again.

Thor picked up the giant and threw him overboard too, to punish him for his cowardice. Then he waded home across the bottom of the sea.

KRISHNA SLAYS THE SERPENT KING

This is the story of how the Hindu god, Krishna, killed the evil serpent king, Kaliya.

As a boy, the blue god, Krishna, lived on the banks of the mighty Yamuna River. Every day cowherds brought their cows to drink from the river and people from the village came to swim. Then one fateful day the serpent king, Kaliya, swam into the river. Now, Kaliya was no ordinary serpent. He had five huge heads, with five sets of poisonous fangs, and coils so strong they could crush you to death. Soon the river was filled with Kaliya's lethal poison. All the fish died, and the trees on the river bank withered and dried up. The cows and cowherds who drank the river water fell down dead. No one dared go near the river – they were too afraid of Kaliya.

A group of cowherds went to visit Krishna.

'You must help us get rid of Kaliya and stop this terror,' they pleaded, 'or there will be no one left.'

'I will save you,' promised Krishna.

Krishna went down to the river and along its deserted banks until he came to its deepest, most poisonous pool. Deadly fumes rose from the water which bubbled and boiled, black and sinister. For this was where Kaliya had made

his home. There was no sign of the serpent, but Krishna knew he was waiting. Krishna climbed up the tallest tree he could find, clapped his hands and plunged into the deadly pool.

The serpent king was, indeed, waiting. As Krishna swam towards him, the snake spun round and round and whipped the water into a mighty whirlpool. Then Kaliya rushed at Krishna, caught him in his crushing coils, and began to squeeze. Krishna stayed quite still and when the serpent relaxed his grip, just for a second, he struggled free and jumped on to Kaliya's five hooded heads. Kaliya hissed and tried to shake him off, but the god was too strong for the snake. Krishna seized one head in one hand and another in the other hand and then he began to dance. He stamped his feet and jumped and kicked. Kaliya felt as if he was being hit with a hundred hammers all at once. His bones began to break under the weight of Krishna's feet.

Kaliya tried to pull one head free and sink his fangs into Krishna's neck, but he was caught fast. Then, all of a sudden, the serpent dived deep into the water, deeper and deeper, to drown Krishna. But Krishna could hold his breath longer than Kaliya, and soon the serpent had to come up again for air.

Krishna took up his punishing dance once again, stamping and stomping on Kaliya's heads, while his friends the cowherds stood on the bank and watched. Soon the pain of the beating made Kaliya very weak. First one head died, then the second, then the third, and the fourth. The fifth head snapped and lunged and spat blood and poison at Krishna. But before very long it, too, gave up the struggle. The serpent king was dead.

Krishna swam back to his friends on the bank who clapped and cheered and thanked him for saving them. And the next day they led their cows down to the river to drink.

THE SHARK GOD LEARNS A LESSON

This story comes from the Fiji islands in the Pacific Ocean.

 Beneath the surface of the turquoise blue sea around Fiji lies a hidden underwater world. The ruler of this world was the great shark god, a huge, quarrelsome creature who was always on the look-out for a fight.

Each of the islands of Fiji had its own guardian, usually a shark that lived in a coral reef nearby. The great shark god considered himself the bravest and strongest of all the guardians. After all, hadn't he often fought the other guardians and won? The other sharks paid tribute to him and did as he told them. Woe betide any of them who dared to challenge his command.

One day, the great shark god was happily patrolling his kingdom when he met an old friend. The friend was a shark god, too, though not so important and not so powerful. But he was very fond of making mischief.

'I've been hearing great things of you,' he said to the great shark god. 'You've been winning all your fights, I'm told.'

'Indeed I have,' the great shark god replied, puffing himself up with pride. 'No one stands a chance against me, I can tell you!'

'Of course they don't, of course they don't,' the friend agreed. 'There's just one thing that puzzles me, I hope you don't mind me saying so?'

'Get on with it, then,' said the great shark god.

'Well, you've never fought the guardian of the Long Island, have you?' said the friend. 'And you're probably wise not to. I mean, everyone else is frightened to death of him. Why risk losing your reputation for the sake of one last fight?'

'What?' roared the great shark god. 'Are you suggesting that I'm afraid to fight? We'll soon see about that!'

And he lashed his tail and sped away, straight towards the Long Island. As he approached the island, he heard a voice coming from the tallest tree. For the first time in his life, a shiver of fear ran down his spine.

'So, you've come to fight at last,' the tree said in a sinister whisper. 'How I wish I could fight you. But I can't leave the land and you can't leave the sea. So it's up to the guardian to fight for me. He will teach you a lesson, and about time too.'

The great shark god swam on towards the reef. Suddenly, a long, curling tentacle shot out of a crack in the coral and grabbed him. Then another and another until he was caught fast and could neither move nor breathe. For the guardian of the Long Island was none other than a giant octopus, with eight giant tentacles. The great shark god had met his match.

The more he struggled, the tighter the octopus pulled until the great shark god felt sure he would die. With his last gasp of breath, and for the first time in his life, he begged for mercy.

'Will you acknowledge me as your master?' the octopus asked.

'Yes, yes!' gasped the great shark god.

'And will you promise never to attack the fishermen of the Long Island and to protect them wherever they go?' continued the octopus.

'I promise! I promise!' wheezed the great shark god.

'Then you can go,' the octopus said and released the great shark god.

The great shark god had learned his lesson. He
was still the bravest and strongest of all the sharks
but he did what the octopus told him, and
guarded the fishermen as they paddled out
to sea. With their own shark to protect
them, no other creatures dared attack
the fishermen of Long Island.

PERSEUS AND THE GORGON

The story of Perseus and his many adventures comes from ancient Greece.

Perseus and his mother, Danae, lived on the island of Seriphos, in the blue Aegean Sea. Perseus's father was Zeus, the king of the gods. Danae was the daughter of Acrisius, king of Argos. When Perseus was born, King Acrisius locked his daughter and grandson in a wooden chest and threw them into the sea. For he had been warned by the gods that Danae's son would kill him. But the chest was washed up safely on the shores of Seriphos and a fisherman took Danae and Perseus to the king of Seriphos, Polydictes.

King Polydictes fell in love with Danae and wanted to marry her – but she refused. Perseus did his best to protect his mother from the king's attentions. But Perseus's devotion only made Polydictes more determined. Polydictes was sure that if he could get rid of Perseus for a while, Danae would quickly change her mind.

One day, Polydictes had an idea. He pretended that he wanted to marry a different princess and invited all the nobles of Seriphos to a sumptuous feast to celebrate his engagement. Each noble was expected to bring a gift for the king. But, as the king suspected, Perseus had nothing to give.

'Then you'll have to perform a great deed, instead,' the king told Perseus.

'Why don't I bring you the head of Medusa the Gorgon?' joked Perseus.

'Good idea!' the king replied, in deadly earnest. 'Off you go!'

Medusa was the daughter of the god of the sea, and she had once been beautiful. But Athene, goddess of wisdom and war, had caught Medusa with her lover. Athene was famous for her short temper, and she immediately transformed Medusa into a hideous monster. Now Medusa had eagle's

wings, claws of bronze, and scales instead of skin. She had two sharp bronze tusks on her face, and writhing snakes, twisting and hissing, instead of hair. Anyone who looked at Medusa's dreadful face was turned to stone. Medusa lived with her sisters, the Gorgons, on a rocky island in the middle of the sea.

With a heavy heart, Perseus set off on his seemingly impossible mission. But the goddess Athene decided to help Perseus destroy the monster that she had created. Athene sent Perseus to three old women, called the Graeae. The Graeae had a single eye and a single tooth between them, which all three used in turn. Perseus stole their one tooth and their one eye and refused to return them until the Graeae told him what he needed to know.

'Go first to the underworld and fetch Pluto's helmet,' they cackled. 'It will make you invisible. Then fetch Hermes' shield and sword. They will be your

weapons. Then take this magic leather bag, and put on these winged sandals. They will help you to fly.' So Perseus took the leather bag and sandals, and went to fetch the helmet, shield and sword.

'One thing more,' the Graeae shrieked, as Perseus prepared to leave. 'Look only at Medusa's reflection in your shield. Never look directly at her face!'

Wearing the helmet of invisibility and the winged sandals, Perseus flew to the island where the Gorgons lived. The three hideous sisters lay asleep. Perseus fixed his eyes on Medusa's reflection in his shining shield, raised his sword and cut off her snake-haired head with one huge stroke. Then he put

her dreadful head into his magic leather bag. The other two Gorgons woke from their sleep and sprang after Perseus with a terrible cry. They rattled their claws and shook their wings but they could not catch him – they could not even see him. As Perseus flew away, drops of Medusa's blood fell to Earth. Some fell on the desert and turned into slithering snakes, and from the others sprang the giant, Chrysaor, and the famous winged horse, Pegasus.

One further adventure lay in wait for Perseus before he finally returned home. As he flew through the sky, he noticed a beautiful girl chained to a rock far below. Her name was Andromeda.

'My father boasted that I was more beautiful than the sea nymphs, ' she sobbed. 'So Poseidon, the sea god, flooded our lands and sent a terrible sea monster to kill our people. The gods told my father to sacrifice me to the monster, or the trouble would never go away.'

'I'll save you,' said Perseus, for he had fallen in love with Andromeda at first sight, 'if you promise to marry me.'

Andromeda promised. Then Perseus lay in wait for the monster to arrive. Suddenly the sea began to foam and a dark shape swam into view. With his helmet of invisibility safely on his head, Perseus swooped down and plunged his sword deep into the monster's shoulder. Soon the sea was stained crimson with the monster's blood. Once the monster was dead, Perseus freed Andromeda from her chains. Then they were married.

When Perseus and Andromeda reached Seriphos, they found Danae in great despair. Polydictes was about to force her to marry him. Perseus told his mother not to worry. He went to Polydictes' court and pulled the head of Medusa the Gorgon out of his bag. As soon as the king and his courtiers looked upon Medusa's face, they were turned into stone. Perseus gave the head to the goddess, Athene, to wear on her war shield.

Perseus, his wife and his mother returned to Danae's real home in Argos. One day, Perseus was taking part in some games when he threw the discus and accidentally killed an old man. The old man was Acrisius, the grand-father Perseus had never met. And so the gods' warning turned out to be true, and Perseus became king in his own right.

THESEUS AND THE MINOTAUR

Theseus was the son of Aegeus, king of Athens. The story of Theseus and his battle with the Minotaur is one of the best-known myths of ancient Greece.

At an early age Theseus proved his strength and courage by killing several terrible giants and monsters. One of these was Sinis, known as Pine-bender, who strapped people between two bent-over pine trees then let the trees go, tearing his victims in two. There was also the brutal Sciron who forced travellers to wash his feet and, as they did so, kicked them into the sea where a huge turtle gobbled them up. Theseus gave Sciron a dose of his own, bitter medicine and hurled him off a cliff.

Now Theseus faced his greatest test – to kill the dreadful Minotaur that lived on the island of Crete. The Minotaur was a hideous monster, with the body of a man and the head and shoulders of a bull. It was savage and blood-thirsty, and thrived on human flesh. The Minotaur lived in an underground maze called the Labyrinth. No one who had ventured into the Labyrinth had ever come out alive.

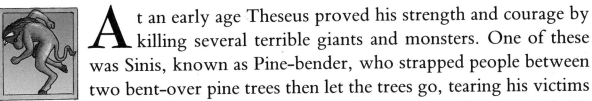

Every nine years the king of Crete, Minos, demanded a tribute of fourteen young Athenians to be thrown to the Minotaur for food. Some years before, King Minos's eldest son had been brutally murdered in Athens and the tribute was Minos's way of avenging his death. As the day of tribute drew close, Athens was plunged into deepest mourning. Theseus went to see his father. He had a plan.

'Father, I will go as one of the fourteen,' he said, as the victims prepared to set sail. 'I will kill the beast and put an end to this terrible tribute for ever.'

King Aegeus was reluctant to let Theseus go and risk his life. But Theseus was determined, and the king agreed, on one condition.

'When you sail away from here, my son,' he said, 'your ships will be flying the black sails of mourning. If, you succeed in killing the Minotaur, hoist white victory sails on your return. Then I will know that you are alive.'

Theseus promised to do as his father requested, and the ship carrying the fourteen Athenians sailed slowly out of the city's harbour.

Now, King Minos had a beautiful daughter, called Ariadne. When she saw Theseus standing among the Minotaur's victims on the quayside in Crete, she fell deeply in love with him. She made up her mind to defy her father, and to help Theseus if he would marry her. Theseus agreed.

'Take this ball of magic ball of string with you,' Ariadne whispered to Theseus. 'When the time comes, it will guide you and your friends safely out of the Labyrinth.'

So Theseus took the ball of string and tied one end to the gate post at the entrance to the Labyrinth. Then, with great trepidation, he followed the other victims into the heart of the dark maze, unravelling the string behind him. From deep in the Labyrinth's centre, came a terrible bellowing. The ground shuddered and shook as the mighty monster stamped its feet. For the Minotaur was hungry and it could smell food. As the first of the Athenians reached its den, the Minotaur reached out to seize him, but Theseus was ready. He pulled out his sword and hacked at the Minotaur's neck and body, covering himself with the Minotaur's blood. His companions cowered against the wall, and watched Theseus fight for their lives. Each time they thought the Minotaur was dead, it reared up its great head and lunged again at Theseus. And each time they thought that the Minotaur had struck Theseus a fatal blow, the prince fought back.

The battle was long and bloody. Finally, with a last surge of energy, Theseus lifted his sword and stuck the Minotaur through the eye. With a dreadful roar, the Minotaur crashed to the ground, dead. Exhausted and reeling from the fight, Theseus picked up the magic string and led his companions out of the Labyrinth.

The Athenians had to make a quick escape from the island of Crete. When King Minos discovered his monster was dead and its victims gone, his anger would know no bounds. Once again, Ariadne came to the Athenians' rescue. She was waiting for them with a boat, and, without further ado, they set sail for Athens and home. On the way, they stopped at the island of Naxos. But while Ariadne slept, Theseus sailed off without her, forgetting all about her and his promise to marry her!

When he saw her abandoned, the god Dionysus took pity on Ariadne and helped her to plot her revenge. Dionysus made Theseus forget another promise – the one he had made to his father. As Theseus sailed home in triumph, he forgot to hoist the white sails of victory. So he entered Athens harbour with the black sails of mourning still flying from his masts. King Aegeus was keeping look-out from the top of a cliff overlooking the harbour, hoping for his son's safe return. When the king saw the black sails he was stricken with grief, for he assumed that his son was dead.

'If my son is dead,' he cried, in despair, 'my own life is not worth living.' And he leapt into the sea and drowned. The sea where he died is still called the Aegean after him.

So Theseus returned home and became the new king of Athens.

SINDBAD THE SAILOR AND THE GIANT ROC

This is one of the stories in the famous Arabian Nights collection.

Long ago, in the city of Baghdad, there lived a poor porter, called Sindbad. One day, as he walked home after a hard, hot day's work, he passed a very grand house with a shady garden full of flowers and fountains. A great feast was going on inside. Sindbad could hear the sounds of singing and laughter and smell the aroma of delicious food.

'Whose house is this?' he asked the gatekeeper.

'Don't you know?' the gatekeeper replied. 'This is the house of Sindbad the Sailor who has travelled round the world and back again!'

'How lucky he is,' the porter sighed. 'I work and work and I never seem to get anywhere.'

Now Sindbad the Sailor heard the porter's words and sent a servant to fetch him. Sindbad the Porter was afraid he would be punished, and trembled with fright. He was led into a great hall where an old man with a long white beard sat at the head of a long table. But Sindbad the Sailor told the porter to take a seat and called for food and drink to be brought for him.

'You are welcome, my friend and my namesake,' Sindbad said. 'Eat and drink, don't be afraid! Then I will tell you a story.'

Sindbad the Porter was never more astonished in his whole life. He ate and drank his fill, and resigned himself to whatever punishment lay in wait. When he had finished, the Sailor spoke again:

'My friend, I heard you complaining about how lucky I am, while you work so hard. I do not blame you for thinking this. But let me say that my good fortune has not come easily. For I travelled the world on seven great voyages, facing death and ruin many times. I will tell you the story of my second voyage.'

'My father was a wealthy merchant and left me a great fortune when he died. But I squandered my money and very soon I had none of it left. So I gave up my home and took to the sea.

'I left Baghdad with a party of merchants and a shipload of goods. A brisk wind sped us on our way and we did excellent trade at each port we visited. One day, we sailed to a beautiful island. No one lived there but we went ashore to refresh ourselves. I sat down under a shady tree and soon I was asleep. Imagine my horror, when I woke up, to find that my companions had sailed away without me! I was all alone with no means of escape.

'Then I noticed a huge, white, shining object lying on the sand nearby. I crept closer and touched it. It was hard and warm and smooth as ivory. As I stood puzzling about what it could be, a great black cloud appeared overhead and blotted out the sun. But this was no ordinary cloud. It was a gigantic bird, called a roc, with legs and feet like tree trunks. And the great white shining thing was its egg. As the mighty bird flew down to the ground, I crept close to its egg so that it covered us both with its enormous wings. Then I tied myself to one of its claws.

' "When it flies away," I told myself, "it will take me away with it."

'All night, the giant roc sat on its egg. Then next morning, as the sun rose, it took off with a mighty flap of its wings, carrying me with it. It soared into the air, higher and higher, then dropped suddenly on to a bare, rocky crag. I quickly untied myself and hid in a crack in the rock.

'When I looked about, I found myself trapped in a deep valley, surrounded by sheer-sided mountains. I was no better off than before! As I walked along the valley, I saw that the ground was sharp and glittering all round, for it was covered in diamonds! I picked up handful upon handful of dazzling diamonds and filled my pockets with them. But as night came the ground began to swarm with hideous snakes, black and thick as tree trunks. I soon decided that I needed to find shelter.

'That night, therefore, I hid in a cave. In the morning I waited until the snakes had returned to their dens before I ventured out again. As I emerged, a great piece of raw meat landed with a thud at my feet. My adventure was growing stranger and stranger. Then I remembered a tale I'd been told about a famous but impassable valley of diamonds and how merchants stole the stones by means of a cunning trick. From the rocks above, they dropped hunks of meat in to the valley, where the sharp diamonds stuck to them. When a roc swooped down to carry the meat to it nest, it carried the diamonds with it. Then the waiting merchants scared away the birds with sticks and stones, and took the diamonds for themselves.

'I never believed this story, until now. Carrying as many of the biggest and best diamonds as I could, I tied myself to a piece of meat and waited for a roc to come and take me to its nest. There, sure enough, two merchants were waiting, though they were surprised and dismayed to see me. I gave a huge diamond to each and asked for their help which they now willingly gave.

'We travelled together until we reached the safety of the port. And then I sailed back home to Baghdad where I lived very well on my new riches, until the time came, that is, for my next adventure . . .'

And with those words, Sindbad the Sailor ended the story of his second great voyage of adventure.

HOW MANTIS STOLE THE FIRE

In African mythology, the praying mantis is a sacred creature that invented words and language, and brought fire to people. This is the story of how the mantis stole the fire. In other African versions of this story, the fire is stolen by a dog, a chimpanzee and a mason wasp.

One day, Mantis smelt a very delicious smell. Ostrich was eating his supper and it smelt very good indeed. Mantis crept as close as he dared and was astonished to find Ostrich roasting his food over a roaring fire. When he had finished eating, Ostrich carefully gathered up the fire and tucked it under his wing for safe-keeping.

Mantis wanted the fire for himself and he needed a trick to get it from Ostrich. He thought long and hard and had an idea.

'Ostrich, oh Ostrich,' he called. 'Come with me. I've found a tree with the most delicious fruit you'll ever taste. Do you want some?'

'Lead the way,' Ostrich replied.

So Mantis led Ostrich to a tree covered in juicy, bright yellow plums and Ostrich happily began to eat. They were the sweetest plums he'd ever tasted.

'Reach a bit higher,' Mantis advised. 'The best fruit is always near the top.'

Ostrich stood on tiptoe and reached up as high as he could, spreading out his wings to help him to balance.

Then Mantis stole the fire from under his wing and ran away as fast as he could. After that, Ostrich never flew again but kept his wings firmly closed.

The story goes that Mantis burned in his own fire and two new Mantises were made from his ashes. One Mantis was shy and quiet. The other was bold and outgoing. One day, the son of bold Mantis was killed by baboons who pulled out his eye. Shy Mantis saw what had happened and fought the baboons to get the eye back. Then he put the eye in water and it grew into a new being, the ancestor of all the human beings now on Earth. And this is how Mantis brought both fire and people to the world.

INDEX